DOGS DON'T WEAR SNEAKERS

# DOGS DON'T WEAR SNEAKERS

## BY LAURA NUMEROFF

### ILLUSTRATED BY JOE MATHIEU

SIMON & SCHUSTER BOOKS FOR YOUNG READERS
Published by Simon & Schuster
New York   London   Toronto   Sydney   Tokyo   Singapore

SIMON & SCHUSTER BOOKS FOR YOUNG READERS
Simon & Schuster Building, Rockefeller Center
1230 Avenue of the Americas, New York, New York 10020
Text copyright © 1993 by Laura Numeroff
Illustrations copyright © 1993 by Joe Mathieu
All rights reserved including the right of reproduction
in whole or in part in any form.
SIMON & SCHUSTER BOOKS FOR YOUNG READERS
is a trademark of Simon & Schuster.
Designed by Vicki Kalajian.
The text of this book is set in 20 point ITC Esprit Book.
The illustrations were done in pencil and dyes.
Manufactured in the United States of America

10   9   8   7   6   5   4

*Library of Congress Cataloging-in-Publication Data*
Numeroff, Laura Joffe.   Dogs don't wear sneakers / by Laura Numeroff ;
illustrated by Joe Mathieu.   p.   cm.   Summary: In a child's
imagination, animals do wacky things, including
ducks riding bikes, yaks skiing, and fish eating bagels.
1. Animals—Juvenile poetry.   2. Children's poetry, American.
[1. Animals—Poetry.   2. Imagination—Poetry.   3. American poetry.]
I. Mathieu, Joseph, ill.   II. Title.   PS3564.U45D63   1993
811'.54—dc20   92-27007   CIP
ISBN: 0-671-79525-2

*To Peanuts, Muffin, and Mandy*
L.N.

*To my mom, Patricia Mathieu*
J.M.

Dogs don't wear sneakers

And pigs don't wear hats

And dresses look silly
On Siamese cats.

Sheep don't take showers
And goats never shave

And you won't find a bathtub
Inside a bear's cave.

Moose don't go bowling

And hens never swim

And you'll never see roosters
Working out in a gym.

Skunks don't ride scooters

And beavers don't skate

HOP IN!

And frogs don't take cabs
When they're out on a date.

# Cows don't go dancing

And yaks never ski

And you won't find a honey bun
Baked by a bee.

Fish don't eat bagels

# And penguins don't teach

And rabbits don't sunbathe
At your local beach.

Now just close your eyes
And draw with your mind.
You might be surprised
At what you will find...

Like parrots in tutus

And lambs selling shoes

And two-story houses
Constructed by gnus,

Or mules painting pictures

And ducks riding bikes

And raccoons with knapsacks
On holiday hikes,

Or bulls flying airplanes

And snails saving twine.

But tell me what you see? It's your dream—not mine!